Kela's Paper Planes

by Anne Giulieri
illustrated by Josh J. O'Brien

Kela was very happy.
Her teacher, Mrs Gee,
had just told the children
about the paper plane contest
at school.

"Mum, I am going to make a paper plane
this weekend," said Kela.
"We will see how far our planes can fly.
And I want mine to be really good!"

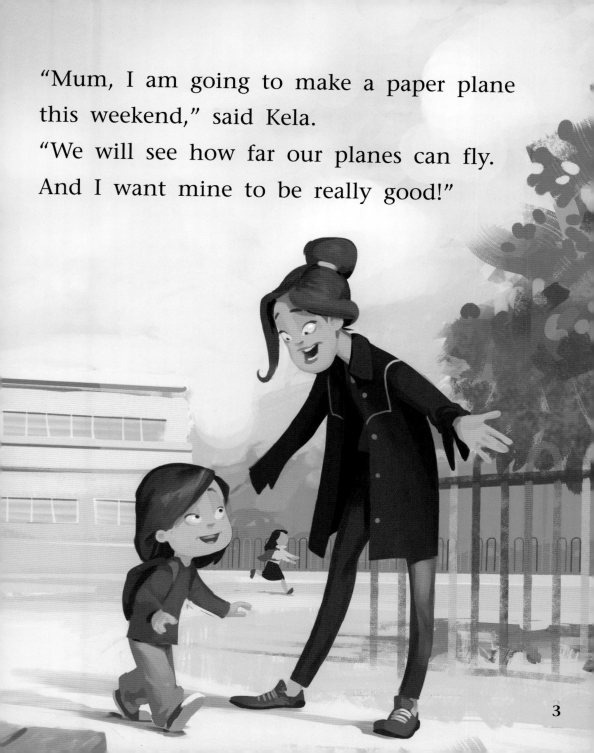

When they got home, Kela got out
her art box and some paper.
"How do I get paper to fly?" thought Kela.
"Paper is flat."

Kela held the paper above her head.
She let it go.
The paper slowly floated to the ground.

Then Kela made the paper into a ball.
She let it go.
But this time, the paper fell quickly
to the floor.

"Mmm," said Kela, as she scratched
her head.
"I'm really going to have
to think about this."

Kela got one more sheet of paper.
This time she carefully folded the paper,
and gave it some wings.
"Look what I have made, Mum!" said Kela.

"It has very long wings and a thin body,"
said Mum.
"Can it fly?"

Kela held the paper above her head.
She let it go.
It span round and round.

"Mmm," thought Kela, as it landed near her feet.
"It stayed in the air, but it didn't go very far.
This is not right.
I will have to keep trying!"

Kela folded some paper.

"This paper plane might fly," said Kela.

"It has a long body and short wings."

"Oh dear," said Kela, as the plane
landed on the floor.

Kela kept trying.
She folded more paper,
but the little plane did not fly far.

Kela wanted to make a plane that could
fly far, and one that was different, too!

"I will go for a walk outside," said Kela.
"It might help me think."

9

As Kela was walking around the garden,
she saw a bird.

The bird went from branch to branch.

Kela carefully looked at its wings
flapping up and down.

"What a pretty bird," thought Kela.

"It has long wings and a long tail."

She looked down and saw a yellow feather.

Kela smiled.

She had a new idea.

The paper plane contest was tomorrow.
And Kela had a lot to do.
She folded the paper into a plane.
She got a pencil and rolled the wings, too.
Her plane was starting to look good now.
"Look at my plane, Mum," said Kela.

"Oh," said Mum.
"That is different!"

The big day had arrived.
Some planes went way, way up,
and some planes went really far.
One plane even did a loop!

"Your turn, Kela," said Mrs Gee.

Kela carefully reached into her box
and pulled out her plane.

"I can tell that you have done
lots of thinking," said Mrs Gee.

"Yes," smiled Kela proudly,
as she sent her plane into the air.

Up, up, up went Kela's plane.
It zoomed through the air.
"Oh, look!" laughed Kela.
"It landed on a branch."

"Well, Kela!" laughed Mrs Gee.
"Your paper plane might not have gone
as far as some of the other planes,
but you did make a wonderful flying bird."

"Yes," laughed Kela.
"And I think my bird made some friends!"
Kela smiled, as all the children laughed.

raintree

a Capstone company — publishers for children

Engage Literacy is published in the UK by Raintree.
Raintree is an imprint of Capstone Global Library Limited, a company
incorporated in England and Wales having its registered office at 264 Banbury
Road, Oxford, OX2 7DY – Registered company number: 6695582

www.raintree.co.uk

Text copyright © Anne Giulieri 2021
Lead authors Jay Dale and Anne Giulieri

Editorial credits
Erika L. Shores, editor; Kayla Rossow, designer; Laura Manthe, production
specialist

Printed and bound in China.

Kela's Paper Planes

ISBN: 978 1 4747 9940 9

Transitional
Level 20
Fiction

Kela needs to make a paper plane.
How can she make paper fly?

raintree
a Capstone company—publishers for children
www.raintree.co.uk

Book Band Level: Purple
ISBN 978-1-4747-9940-9

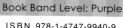

9 781474 799409

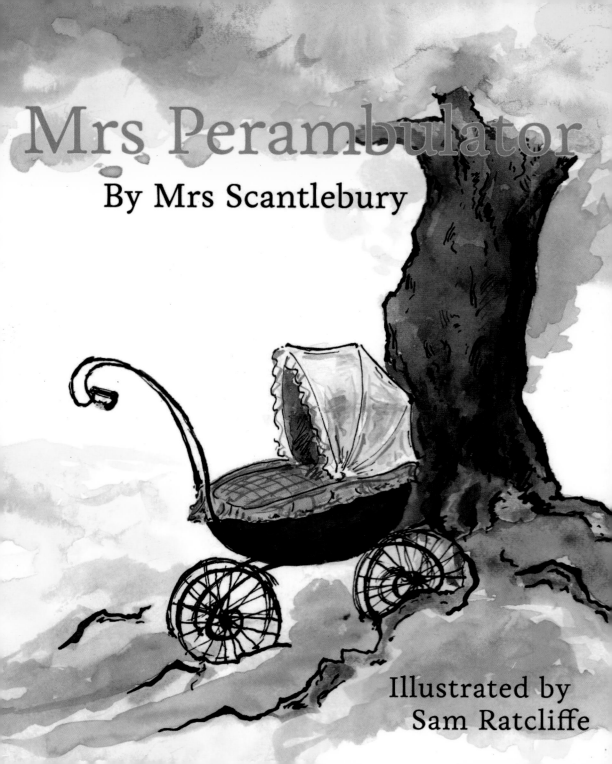

Mrs Perambulator

Design and Illustration by Sam Ratcliffe

Published in 2012 by Ann Scantlebury.
© Ann Scantlebury
ISBN 978-0-9574800-0-1